LEGO STAR WARS™

ULTIMATE STICKER BOOK
DARTH VADER'S EMPIRE

How to use this book

Read the captions, then find the
sticker that best fits the space.
(Hint: check the sticker labels for clues!)

•

Don't forget that your stickers can be
stuck down and peeled off again.

•

There are lots of fantastic extra
stickers for creating your own
scenes throughout the book.

LONDON, NEW YORK,
MELBOURNE, MUNICH AND DELHI

Written by Shari Last
Edited by Garima Sharma
Designed by Lauren Rosier and Suzena Sengupta
Jacket designed by Suzena Sengupta
DTP Designer Umesh Singh Rawat

First published in Great Britain in 2014
by Dorling Kindersley Limited
80 Strand, London WC2R 0RL

10 9 8 7 6 5 4 3 2 1
001–257110–May/14

LEGO, the LEGO logo, the Brick and Knob configurations
and the Minifigure are trademarks of the LEGO Group.
© 2014 The LEGO Group
Produced by Dorling Kindersley under licence from the LEGO Group.

© 2014 Lucasfilm Ltd & ™.
All rights reserved. Used under authorisation.

Page design copyright © 2014 Dorling Kindersley Limited
A Penguin Random House Company

A CIP catalogue record for this book is available from the British Library.

ISBN: 978-1-40935-365-2

Colour reproduction by Alta Image, UK
Printed and bound by L-Rex Printing Co., Ltd, China

Discover more at
www.dk.com
www.LEGO.com
www.starwars.com

TWO SIDES OF THE GALAXY

The galaxy is in a state of unrest after the heroic Jedi were defeated by the evil Sith. Emperor Palpatine has taken control of the galaxy and turned it into an evil Sith Empire. However, a small group of rebels and one Jedi Knight are determined to destroy the Sith and bring peace and happiness back to the galaxy.

DARTH VADER
Darth Vader leads the Imperial Army of the evil Empire. He is feared by everyone in the galaxy – including his own soldiers!

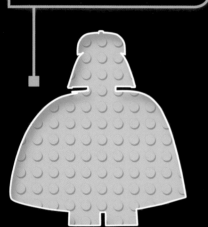

IMPERIAL OFFICER
Imperial officers work on the huge battle station, the Death Star. They operate the computers, fire the cannons and help plan the Empire's next move.

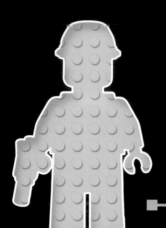

STORMTROOPER
All the soldiers of the Empire wear identical white armour and carry deadly blasters. Rebels, beware!

BOBA FETT
The most famous bounty hunter in the galaxy, Boba Fett is fast and fierce. He is hired by Darth Vader to capture Han Solo.

DEATH STAR GUNNER
Thousands of Death Star gunners are trained to defend the Death Star from rebel attacks.

LEIA

Princess Leia is a senator from Alderaan. She is on a mission to bring peace and justice to the galaxy.

LUKE SKYWALKER

Luke Skywalker is a Jedi Knight – and the secret son of Darth Vader. Will Luke choose the path of the light side or the dark side?

IMPERIAL MIGHT

The Empire uses huge Star Destroyer ships to travel the galaxy and enforce Imperial rule.

MON MOTHMA

Mon Mothma is one of the leaders of the Rebel Alliance. She will try her hardest to end the rule of the Empire.

LANDO CALRISSIAN

Gambler Lando Calrissian chooses to join the Rebel Alliance. He does not want the Empire to remain in control of the galaxy.

HAN SOLO

Han Solo is the pilot of the starship *Millennium Falcon*. He joins the rebels in many space battles, and helps them fight the Imperial Army.

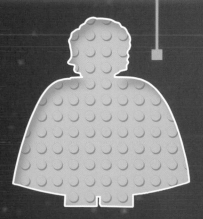

CAPTURED BY JABBA

Jabba the Hutt is a dangerous and powerful criminal who lives on the planet Tatooine. He often holds people captive until he gets what he wants. Jabba is not a Jedi or a Sith, but he joins forces with whichever side will benefit him, the most. When Jabba captures Han Solo, he finds himself battling against the rebels.

MAX REBO
Max Rebo is the lead musician in the Max Rebo Band. The band is forced to play music for Jabba in exchange for food.

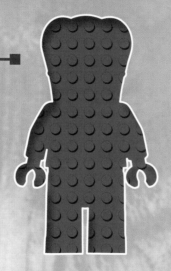

HAN IN CARBONITE
Han Solo causes Jabba so much trouble that the crime lord captures and freezes him in a substance called carbonite.

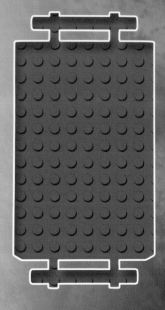

OOLA
Oola is a Twi'lek dancer. She thought dancing for Jabba would be a good job, but she was wrong! Now she can never leave.

PRINCESS LEIA
Princess Leia tries to rescue her friend Han Solo, but she is captured às well! Now Leia is chained to Jabba himself.

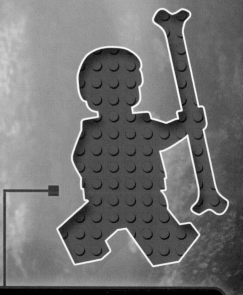

JEDI PRISONER
Jabba is excited because he has captured Luke Skywalker, a Jedi. But it is a trick – Luke wants to be caught so he can free Han and Leia.

Use your extra stickers to create your own scene.

RANCOR
This monster lives in a pit under Jabba's palace. Stay away – he is very dangerous!

BATTLE OF YAVIN

The Imperial Army has found the secret rebel base on the moon Yavin 4. The rebels must defend their base and destroy the Empire's deadly weapon, the Death Star. Rebel pilots soar through space in battle formation, but the Imperial fleet is in attack position, too. The battle is about to begin!

JEDI PILOT
Luke is an amazing pilot. He flies his X-wing along the surface of the Death Star, looking for the best spot to attack.

REBEL STARFIGHTER
X-wings are the best ships in the rebel fleet. They have four wings, four laser cannons and a defence shield.

DEATH STAR
The Death Star is a moon-sized battle station, built by Emperor Palpatine.

VADER'S TIE FIGHTER
Darth Vader's TIE fighter is no ordinary starship. It has a strong hull and an accurate weapons targeting system.

PILOT VADER
Darth Vader flies his TIE fighter behind Luke's X-wing. Will Vader be able to match Luke's piloting skills?

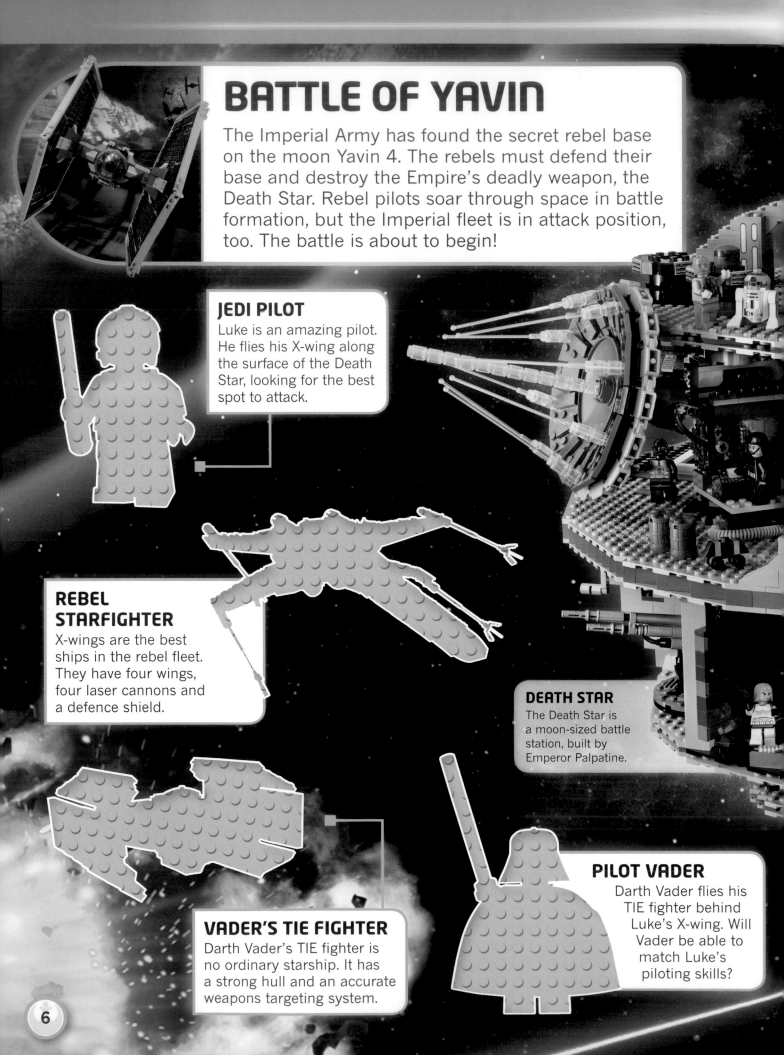

DEATH STAR CANNON

Thousands of cannons on the surface of the Death Star fire their lasers into space. Will they hit their rebel targets?

Y-WING

Y-wings are fast, sturdy rebel ships that carry lots of proton torpedoes. Their target is the Death Star. Can they destroy it?

GOLD LEADER

Dutch Vander is "Gold Leader", the commander of Gold Squadron. He leads a formation of Y-wings into battle against the Imperial fleet.

MILLENNIUM FALCON

Flying the *Millennium Falcon*, Han Solo attacks Darth Vader's TIE fighter and helps Luke to destroy the Death Star.

BATTLE OF HOTH

Concealed on the barren, icy plains of the planet Hoth is Echo Base, the new headquarters of the Rebel Alliance. But it won't stay hidden for long. Darth Vader and his army are on their way to Hoth – and they are going to launch a devastating ground assault! Can the rebels defend their base?

PROBE DROID

Darth Vader sends probe droids to find out where the rebels are hiding. One of them tracks down the rebels on Hoth.

GENERAL VEERS

Imperial officer General Veers leads the attack on Echo Base. He is an expert on AT-AT walkers.

GENERAL RIEEKAN

General Rieekan is a clever rebel leader. He directs his troopers and helps them to avoid enemy fire.

P-TOWER TURRET

Blast away at the Imperial snowtroopers! The P-Tower turret swivels so it can fire powerful laser beams at approaching enemies.

SNOWTROOPERS

Vader's snowtroopers zip lightly over snow on their small, fast speeders. Watch out!

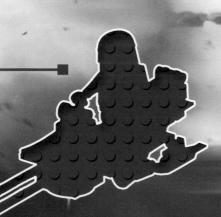

AT-AT WALKER

The enormous All Terrain Armoured Transport (AT-AT) machines are very scary. They are advancing towards the rebel troopers. Help!

SNOWSPEEDER

There's only one way to defeat an AT-AT! Luke flies his snowspeeder around the huge walker's legs, tripping it up with a heavy cable.

HAN ON HOTH

Han Solo loves the warm sandy beaches of his home planet Corellia – he doesn't like the icy wastelands of Hoth. Brrr!

LEADER LEIA

Princess Leia plans battle strategies with rebel generals and officers at Echo Base.

READY, AIM, FIRE!

Rebel troopers on Hoth are ready to defend their base.

UNDERCOVER!

It looks like some of our heroes have decided to join forces with the Empire. But they have actually chosen the opposite! These brave adventurers are working undercover to rescue their friends from danger. They wear disguises to confuse their enemies. Will their cunning missions succeed?

STORMTROOPER LUKE

Has Luke joined the Imperial Army? No – he has disguised himself as a stormtrooper so he can enter the Death Star prison level undetected.

BOUSHH

Has Boushh the bounty hunter brought Jabba a prisoner? No – it's Princess Leia in disguise! She is on a mission to save Han Solo.

STORMTROOPER HAN

Han Solo also wears stormtrooper armour. He is helping Luke rescue Princess Leia from Darth Vader on the Death Star.

WOOKIEE PRISONER

Chewbacca hasn't really been captured… he's pretending to be handcuffed so he can enter Jabba's palace and save Han!

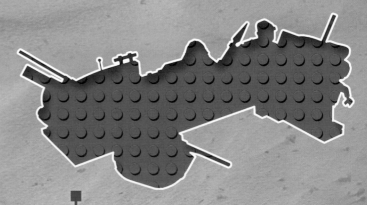

LANDO THE GUARD

Lando wears the uniform of one of Jabba's guards. But he's waiting to reveal his identity and save Luke.

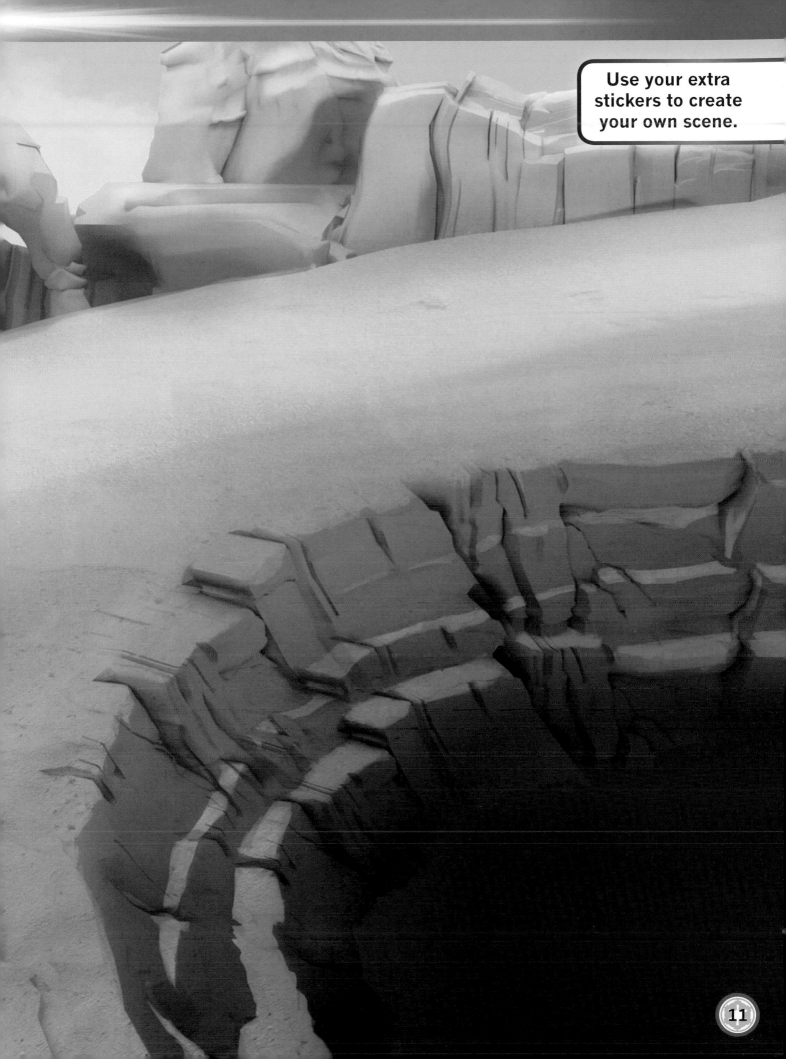

Use your extra stickers to create your own scene.

TREETOP ADVENTURE

Deep in the forests on the moon of Endor, a tribe of Ewoks live in a treetop village. Their quiet planet has been invaded by the Imperial Army and the rebels have arrived to confront them. The Ewoks have a choice: should they join the stormtroopers or the rebels?

LEIA ON ENDOR
Princess Leia is welcomed by the Ewok tribe. The Ewoks give her a dress made from materials from their village.

CAUGHT BY EWOKS
The Ewoks have made Luke their prisoner. Can he use the Force to persuade the small, furry warriors to help the rebels?

WICKET
Wicket is a friendly young Ewok. He meets Princess Leia in the forest and rescues her from a stormtrooper.

TREETOP VILLAGE
Ewoks build their villages in trees to protect them from intruders.

HAN IN DANGER
The Ewoks are going to roast Han Solo on a spit over the fire! How will Han get out of this tough spot?

IMPERIAL SPEEDER BIKE
Imperial stormtroopers patrol the forests of Endor. They ride super-fast speeder bikes, but the Ewoks have a plan to stop them.

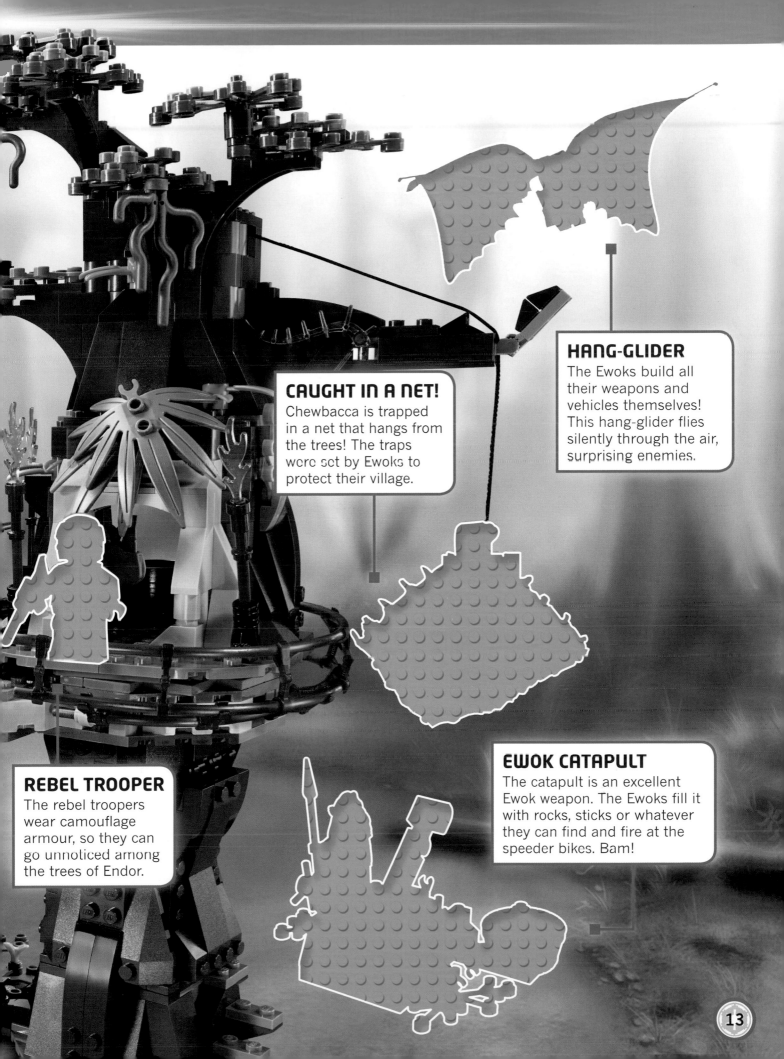

HANG-GLIDER
The Ewoks build all their weapons and vehicles themselves! This hang-glider flies silently through the air, surprising enemies.

CAUGHT IN A NET!
Chewbacca is trapped in a net that hangs from the trees! The traps were set by Ewoks to protect their village.

REBEL TROOPER
The rebel troopers wear camouflage armour, so they can go unnoticed among the trees of Endor.

EWOK CATAPULT
The catapult is an excellent Ewok weapon. The Ewoks fill it with rocks, sticks or whatever they can find and fire at the speeder bikes. Bam!

BATTLE OF ENDOR

The Empire has built a second deadly Death Star! The rebels want to destroy it, so they can defeat the Empire once and for all. But the Death Star is protected by the Imperial fleet. Can the rebels destroy the Death Star with their fleet of small ships? The fate of the galaxy will be decided by this space battle.

TIE FIGHTER

Hundreds of TIE fighters swarm out of the Death Star and begin firing their laser cannons. Can the rebels dodge them?

DEADLY LASER

The Death Star's laser beam can destroy an entire planet!

A-WING

The A-wing is one of the fastest starships in the galaxy. It flies swiftly, avoiding the Imperial TIE fighters.

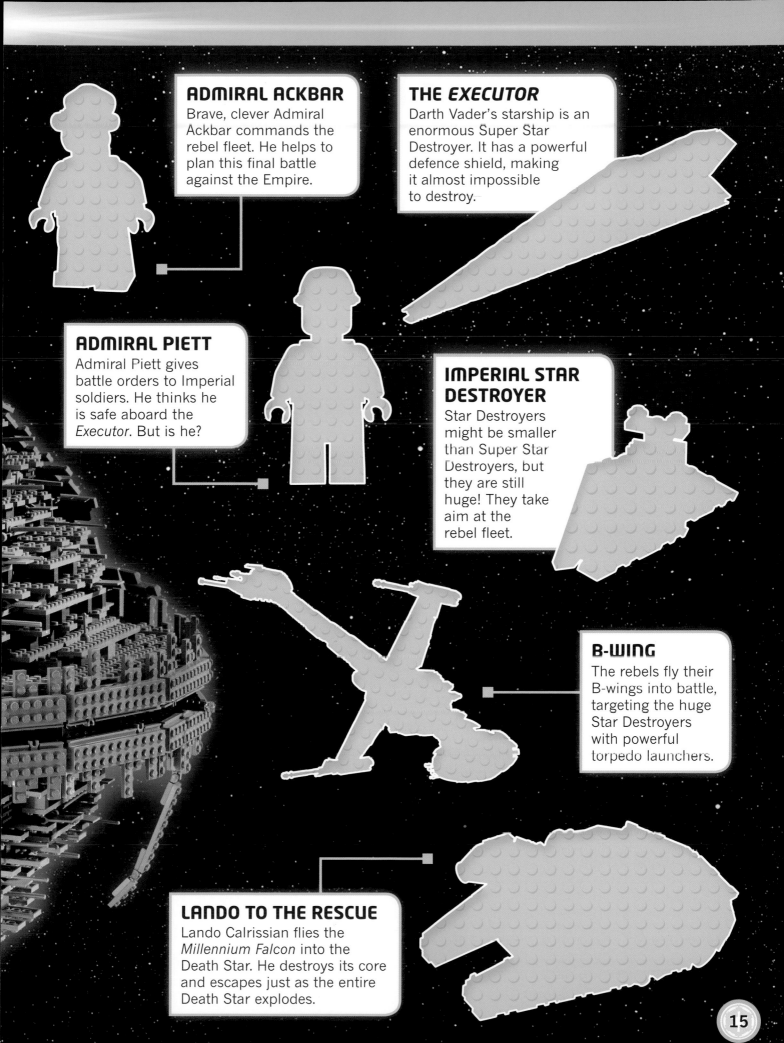

ADMIRAL ACKBAR

Brave, clever Admiral Ackbar commands the rebel fleet. He helps to plan this final battle against the Empire.

THE *EXECUTOR*

Darth Vader's starship is an enormous Super Star Destroyer. It has a powerful defence shield, making it almost impossible to destroy.

ADMIRAL PIETT

Admiral Piett gives battle orders to Imperial soldiers. He thinks he is safe aboard the *Executor*. But is he?

IMPERIAL STAR DESTROYER

Star Destroyers might be smaller than Super Star Destroyers, but they are still huge! They take aim at the rebel fleet.

B-WING

The rebels fly their B-wings into battle, targeting the huge Star Destroyers with powerful torpedo launchers.

LANDO TO THE RESCUE

Lando Calrissian flies the *Millennium Falcon* into the Death Star. He destroys its core and escapes just as the entire Death Star explodes.

BATTLESHIPS

The Imperial and rebel fleets have to consider many things before building or selecting their starships. Size, firepower, manoeuvrability and speed are all important. But different ships have different strengths. Which starfighters are the best for a deadly space battle?

TIE INTERCEPTOR
These arrowlike starfighters are perfect for a fierce space battle. They are fast and manoeuvrable because of their small size.

X-WING
X-wings are bigger than TIE Interceptors, but they are still extremely fast. They also have a lot of firepower and a strong defence system.

IMPERIAL SHUTTLE
This luxurious ship transports Emperor Palpatine across the galaxy in safety.

CARGO SHIP
The *Millennium Falcon* is a cargo ship. It is not built for war, although it has been involved in many. Despite its large size, it is very fast and easy to manoeuvre.

STAR DESTROYER
Star Destroyers are huge Imperial starships. They have an enormous amount of firepower, but they are slow and clumsy during a space battle.

Max Rebo

Rebel Starfighter

Pilot Vader

Jabba's Rancor

Han On Hoth

Luke's Droid

R5-J2

Wicket

Mon Mothma

Battle Station

Droid Slave

A-Wing

Ben Kenobi

Ewok

Ewoks And C-3PO

Leia On Endor

GNK Droid

Cargo Ship

Rebel Trooper

Hoth Rebel

Princess Leia

Droid

Jedi Pilot

Sandcrawler

Death Star Gunner

Enemy Machine

Scout Trooper

Probe Droid

Lando Calrissian

Emperor's Ship

Endor

Wookiee Prisoner

Snowtroopers

Jabba The Hutt

Brave Wookiee

Jedi Prisoner

Vader's Starship

Han Solo

AT-AT Driver

Star Destroyer

Boba Fett

Chewbacca Takes Control!

Rebel

Leader Leia

Coruscant

General Veers

Imperial Star Destroyer

AT-AT Walker

Sith Trooper

Hoth Bunker

Jawa

Oola

Tatooine

X-Wing

Briefing Room

Hang-Glider

Imperial Officer

Jabba's Band

Wampa

Tauntaun

Stormtrooper Luke

R5-A7

Rotta

Ewok Catapult

Salacious Crumb

Lando To The Rescue

Admiral Ackbar

Battle Weapon

Han In Carbonite

Jedi Cruiser

General Rieekan

Death Star Cannon

Snowspeeder

Leia

Rebel Han

B-Wing

Caught by Ewoks

Lando The Guard

Ewok Chief

Old Ben Kenobi

Imperial Pilot

Jabba's Sail Barge

©2014 LEGO